To Frank Baker, Nevada buckaroo
1911–1990
A.H.S.

To Ted Baker and his grandson Brett,
with thanks
T. L.

Clarion Books   a Houghton Mifflin Company imprint, 215 Park Avenue South, New York, NY 10003. Text copyright © 1993 by Ann Herbert Scott.
Illustrations copyright © 1993 by Ted Lewin. All rights reserved. For information about permission to reproduce selections from this book, write
to Permissions, Houghton Mifflin Company, 215 Park Avenue South, New York, NY 10003. For information about this and other Houghton Mifflin
trade and reference books and multimedia products, visit The Bookstore at Houghton Mifflin on the World Wide Web at
(http://www.hmco.com/trade/). Printed in Italy.
Library of Congress Cataloging-in-Publication Data. Scott, Ann Herbert. Cowboy Country / Ann Herbert Scott ; pictures by Ted Lewin.   p.   cm.
Summary: An "old buckaroo" tells how he became a cowboy, what the work was like in the past, and how this life has changed.   ISBN 0-395-57561-3
PA ISBN 0-395-76482-3   1. Cowboys—West (U.S.)—Juvenile literature.   2. West (U.S.)—Social life and customs—Juvenile literature.   [1. Cowboys.
2.West (U.S.)—Social life and customs.]   I. Lewin, Ted, ill.   II. Title.   F596.S29   1993   978'.0092'2—dc20 CIP   AC

NWI 10 9 8 7 6 5 4

Cowboy Country

ANN HERBERT SCOTT   Pictures by TED LEWIN

CLARION BOOKS
New York

You say you've never been to cowboy country
and you'd like to take a look.
It's good you have a day or two to spare.
I see you've brought your backpack.
Stow it here beside Matilda.
This old dog and I'll be proud to take you there.

We'll head out beyond the city,
past the fast foods and the billboards
to where you can see the mountains
cutting their teeth against the sky.

We'll stop by the ranch for the horses
and my old pack mule Eliza.
We won't need much—cowboys travel light.

You say you've never met a real cowboy before?
Well, I guess I'm about as real
as an old buckaroo can get.
I grew up in this country—
my grandparents homesteaded this ranch—
and I've been riding ever since I can remember.

I was helping my dad round up cattle
when I was a lot younger than you are now,
watching my uncles break wild horses,
listening to the stories of rustlers
and mean old bulls and wrecks in rodeo rides,
when we camped beside the cattle
out there in the sagebrush
where the wind sings to the coyotes
and the coyotes sing to the moon.

This little pinto pony will take good care of you.
Sugar knows these trails and knows these cows,
and she's surefooted as a mountain goat.

Eliza here has hauled my gear for many a year.
She's followed me through blizzards where
I couldn't see beyond my horse's ears
and thunderstorms where lightning set the trees on fire.

We've camped out on the desert for weeks on end—
ninety miles from a telephone with nothing
but the wind and sun and stars to keep us company.

Let's go, we're burning daylight.
You and Sugar follow Buck and me.
We'll head for Devil's Canyon.
We should make it there by dark.
We can check the cattle all along the way.

You think you'd like to learn to cowboy?
Then you'll need to watch and listen.
Most cowboys don't say much
but their eyes and ears are working all the time.
See that old cow lying on her side in the willows?
She may be asleep, but on the other hand
she could have run a thorn into her hoof.
Let's check her out. Right here by my saddle
I carry a kit for doctoring.
You don't need to be a vet
to give a sick calf a shot
or swab out a cut or treat a cow for worms.

See that bull over by the boulder?
I think he belongs to our neighbors
over beyond Lone Mountain.
Let's check his brand.
They trucked that critter all the way from Canada.
I know they wouldn't want to lose him now.

Do the cattle all look the same to you?
Well, they're just as different as people are
when you take the care to know them.
If you've seen western movies
or watched cowboys on TV,
you might guess it's bronc riding
and roping snorting steers that makes a top hand.
Well, you'd guess wrong.

Of course, any good buckaroo needs to know
how to handle a rough pony and slip a slick noose,
but it's reading cows that makes a good cowboy—
knowing what an old cow is thinking
before she knows herself. It takes years
to learn that—maybe a lifetime—
but you're starting young,
and you've got lots of time.

Let's stop for a minute beside these aspen trees.
They call this place Indian Springs.
Shoshone people made their campfires here.
If you look sharp you'll find some chips
of black obsidian or quartz, or maybe
a spear point or arrowhead. Years back
the Indians made their way on foot,
gathered the wild seeds, fished the streams for trout,
and trapped jackrabbits in the nets they wove.

That was before the horse and white man came
to change it all. These days
lots of Indian people ranch and buckaroo.
You should see some of those Shoshone cowboys—
they ride like a hole in the wind.

How're you holding up? You've had quite a ride.
Let's make camp here before we lose the sun.
I'll unpack Eliza and take care of the horses
while you round up some sagebrush for a fire.
Tonight you can help me play cookie.
You scrub the spuds beside the stream
and I'll rustle up a pot of cowboy stew.

Taste good? Must be you're hungry.
Here, have another helping. You, too, Matilda.
It'll be a while till breakfast.
    So your teacher said she didn't believe
there were any real cowboys left.
Well, you could say she's right
if by *cowboys* she means those oldtime cattlemen
who drove the giant herds north
from Texas range to Kansas railroad yards,
pushing those squirrely Longhorns
a thousand miles or more.

My grandfather's grandfather cowboyed then—
months without a bath or drink
or sight of a woman's face.
No wonder they went wild when they hit town!

The farmers put an end to all that,
stringing their barbed wire across the dusty trails,
planting their wheat and corn in neat square fields
where cowboys used to ride night herd
and race the cattle in the great stampedes.

The times *have* changed. Your teacher's right on that.
When I was a young buckaroo in these Nevada hills,
a man could ride all day without a fence to cross.
Now highways and barbed wire cut up the range,
and trucks and tractors do the work
of many a good old team.
Rich ranchers use airplanes to round up cattle in the fall
and home computers to keep their records straight.

The government tells us how to run the range,
and women don't stay in the kitchen anymore.
  Don't get me wrong. The changes aren't all bad.
Some of these cowgirls are top hands.
I watch them herding cattle, doctoring calves,
pitching in around the fire at branding time.
And as for trucks, I'd be the first to say
a pickup comes in handy when you're miles from town.

Sure, times have changed. But on the whole
things don't change all that much.
When it comes to handling cattle, to roping,
branding, checking stock, pushing a herd to pasture,
there's nothing anywhere to beat a rider and a horse.

After all, the critters stay about the same—
a cow bogged down in mud up to her ears,
an ornery old bull charging through the brush,
a frightened calf roped for the branding fire.

The weather doesn't change that much either.
And it's the weather that gets you in the end—
the big winters when the blizzards work overtime
and the ice chokes the water holes,
and even the stoutest team and sleigh
can't make it through the drifts to bring the hay
to feed the freezing cows before they die.

Maybe the worst is drought.
A man can stand the heat
as long as there's water in the streams
and browse for livestock on the range.
But when month follows month without a rain,
and grass burns up and brush turns dry
and thirsty cattle roam in search of springs,
then cowboys watch the sky and pray.
Times like that can make a buckaroo cry.

This old bedroll of mine has been through it all.
I've been out on the desert when it was thirty-five below
with nothing but this bedroll and the snow—
no shack, no tent, no trailer. So cold
I bundled up in every shirt I owned
and used an axe to shave my supper
from a frozen slab of beef.
This bedroll is my bunk, my closet, my chest of drawers,
a stout canvas roof to pull over my head.
There's room for Matilda to stretch out across my chest,
space for clean socks, an extra shirt,
my war bag with my dad's old spurs,
a book of poems, a bunch of harness bells,
and enough quilts to soften
the territory between me and the rocks.

On a night like this you can understand
why I wouldn't trade my life for any man's.
It's worth the cold and sweat and dust
just to lie back and watch the stars
come blazing their own trail across the sky,
and listen to the stream's song and the hoot owl's cry,
and wake to coyotes singing in the hills.

So you've made up your mind?
You're going to try your hand at cowboying?
Then you'll be back again.
I guess I'd better warn you—
if you're looking for a ranch job,
you'll need to bring along some gear of your own:
a saddle and a bridle, a throwing rope, a bedroll,
maybe a slicker for the rain.
You'll have to pack a shoeing outfit,
and you'd better know how to use it—
you'll have to shoe your own horses
when you're out there on the range.

Learn all you can of horses before you leave home,
and it wouldn't be a bad idea
to get acquainted with a cow.
Watch the old buckaroos.
They know the business in their bones.

Keep your eyes open and your mouth mostly shut
and you'll catch on—that's how we all began.
You're lucky to be starting out.
I wish I was your size.
I guess you know
I'd do it all again.